JAN. 31

ALSO BY ALBERT GOLDBARTH

PAMPHLET
Under Cover (The Best Cellar Press, 1973)

BOOKS
Coprolites (New Rivers Press, 1973)
Opticks (Seven Woods Press, 1974)

JAN. 31

by Albert Goldbarth

1974
DOUBLEDAY & COMPANY, INC.
GARDEN CITY, NEW YORK

Library of Congress Cataloging in Publication Data

Goldbarth, Albert.
Jan. 31.
Poems.

I. Title.
PS3557.O354J3   811'.5'4
ISBN 0-385-05955-8 Trade
  0-385-06085-8 Paperbound
Library of Congress Catalog Card Number 73-22534

Grateful acknowledgment is made by the author to the editors of the following publications, where many of these poems first appeared, for permission to reprint.

"Hard Times" first appeared in *Poetry Northwest* © 1973 by the University of Washington; "Song For Natural Defenses" in *The Midwest Quarterly* © 1973 by *The Midwest Quarterly*; "Three Anatomical Points" in *The Ohio Review* © 1973 by Ohio University; "Tidings" in *The Midwest Quarterly* © 1973 by *The Midwest Quarterly*; "The Class Of 65" in *Shenandoah* © 1974 by *Shenandoah*; "Through The State" in *Concerning Poetry*; "People Are Dropping Out Of Our Lives" in *The Falcon* © 1972 by Mansfield State College; "Warning The Crowd" in *West Coast Poetry Review* © 1974 by *West Coast Poetry Review*; "Against The Odor" in *Poetry Northwest* © 1972 by the University of Washington; "Self-Protection" excerpted from *Opticks*, a book-length poem published by Seven Woods Press © 1974 by Albert Goldbarth; "Becoming Landscape" in *Three Rivers Poetry Journal* © 1974 by Three Rivers Press; "Intercourse In Bad Weather" in *The Midwest Quarterly* © 1973 by *The Midwest Quarterly*; "The Always" in *The Dragonfly* © 1974 by *The Dragonfly*; "Poem" in *Poetry Northwest* © 1972 by the University of Washington; "Song For Longing" in *Carolina Quarterly* © 1973 by *Carolina Quarterly*; "Duty" in *North American Review* © 1973 by the University of Northern Iowa; "How To Keep Warm In February" in *The Antioch Review* © 1973 by The Antioch Review, Inc.; "Death And Resurrection Through Glass" excerpted from *Opticks*, a book-length poem published by Seven Woods Press © 1974 by Albert Goldbarth; "Married In The Presence Of The Lord" in *The Antioch Review* © 1973 by The Antioch Review, Inc.; "Kartoon Kapers" in *Modern Poetry Studies* © 1974 by Jerome Mazzaro; "Pact" in *The Midwest Quarterly* © 1973 by *The Midwest Quarterly*; "Song For Pure Direction" in *Poetry Northwest* © 1972 by the University of Washington; "The Disaster Tree" in *The Iowa Review* © 1974 by the University of Iowa; "Flux" in *The Antioch Review* © 1973 by The Antioch Review, Inc.; "Car Radio" in *The Antioch Review* © 1974 by The Antioch Review, Inc.; "Nostalgia" in *The Dragonfly* © 1974 by *The Dragonfly;* "The Stories": Part 1, "Grown" in *Poetry Now* © 1973 by E. V. Griffith, Part 2, "Linda's," in *Kansas Quarterly* © 1971 by *Kansas Quarterly;* "The Concept Of Voice In Fiction" in *Epoch* © 1972 by Cornell University; "Handicaps" in *The Antioch Review* © 1973 by The Antioch Review, Inc.; "Letter To Friends East And West" in *CutBank* © 1973 by ASUM; "A Winter Minimal" in *Seizure;* "Piscary Poem" in *The Ark River Review* © 1973 by *The Ark River Review;* "The First Amendment To The Constitution Of The United States" in *Poetry Northwest* © 1973 by the University of Washington; "How We Met" in *Dacotah Territory* © 1973 by *Dacotah Territory;* "The Poem That Doesn't Look Like Much" in *Carolina Quarterly* © 1973 by *Carolina Quarterly;* "The Bittersweet Comfort Of Motley Detail" in *Poetry* © 1973 by the Modern Poetry Association; "Straddling The Banks" in *The Nation* © 1972 by The Nation Associates, Inc.; "Survival" in *Poetry* © 1971 by The Modern Poetry Association; "Poem To Comfort My Sister" in *The Beloit Poetry Journal* © 1973 by *The Beloit Poetry Journal;* "Field" in *The Ohio Review* © 1972 by Ohio University.

Thanks, also, for permission to reprint lines from James Taylor's song FIRE AND RAIN © 1969 by Blackwood Music Inc. and Country Music Inc.

for Chicago friends

Lord knows
When the cold wind blows
It'll turn your head around
JAMES TAYLOR

Special thanks to The Best Cellar Press for including some of these poems in the pamphlet *Under Cover,* and to Seven Woods Press for originally publishing "Self-Protection" and "Death And Resurrection Through Glass" as units of a book-length poem, *Opticks.* Extra thanks too to Carolyn Stoloff for her impetus.

CONTENTS

NOTE

The poems in this loosely organized sequence are meant as a diary-of-sorts kept through one metaphorical winter, and are concerned with ways of surviving through that period. Although a casual progression is intended, from preparation for the season, through attrition following the season's start, to a final winning of minimal survival at the season's end, this ordering is not intended to be rigid. Some of the poems are intended to act as flashback, prophecy, and conjecture, to approximate a sense of spontaneous notation through difficult times.

Lhude sing Goddamm
POUND

JAN. 31

HARD TIMES

1.
Faucets
hover over the sink
like the short-sleeves
of an amputee
remembering what it was
to wash up.
*
These are hard times
in Chicago, darling.

2.
Winters like this freeze
anything shining
to anything unbuttoned.
Hard times.
The lonely man's neck
must wait for spring
to thaw the knife-blade
out of the cut
across his eager fingers.
*
Ice. The infant gums
and tongues some warmth
about the blue ankle
trapped
in the frozen baptism,
beats his head against ice
for the foot bloated
belly-up within.

1

Hard times. Ice. You could claw
a hole in the tear
glazed over your cheek
and fish
with my heart on a hook
for your sorrow.

*

Ice in Chicago. Darling,
hard times. Anything wet
becomes monumental.
The lonely man
haunts the streets with an egg
of semen
cracked in the palm of his hand.

3.

I need you. By the way
my fingers travel
over the swells of you
like refugees
leaving America
I know. The thumb
is blind from birth.
It bends
its head to the ground
and moves
by what it hears there.

*

A time of need.
Voices in a telephone cable
twine without touching.
Lovers too
have been known
to keep rubber between them.

2

Ice:
words in a wire
die of cold
waiting outside
for their ring to be answered.

*

I need you
to say: to a herbivore
the whole world's a salad.
You're silly
like that. I need to feel your breasts
burn like bulbs.
And we need the bulbs.
They make their own light

*

and we do with them,
in a hard time,
for cherubim.

3

SONG FOR NATURAL DEFENSES

Anything helps. The eyelid covers the eye
more often per minute, you can't see
the change, but it's there, it helps.
The eardrum's that much thicker, maybe
having learned from the thumbnail
thoughts of what it would be like to hear

after death; well, we're not dead; and it's not
a nail; and yet is more, by that much, a nail.
That helps. The nerve-ends under the old
shell game, the elbows, clang against almost
any surface; but not any; once, they jangled in rumors
of wind; now it takes the wind. The urine is heavy

tea color, teeth root in around a ball of gum
enough to encapsulize it, this helps, extra fat
in my cheek absorbs your kiss before my brain
receives the message. It's not a happy time,
this getting ready for winter, but necessary.
They say, up North, this year the snow is this much

more like stone. And if the heart goes bone
by one cell, well, we can't help that.

THREE ANATOMICAL POINTS

1.

I know it's morning by silk
straining small gold curds of sun
into the black borsht of my slumber,
a soup served chilled, a night dish.
Morning is parting the drapes
to what's warm. Or maybe, in a field
of white lupine, there's a mare out to pasture
spreading her buttocks
for one last shaft of heat
through the glassy cold of the coming season.

2.

Linen could be abrasive
here. My own tongue's rough as a cat's,
wants to lap like a cat's; but only the air
is allowed to suck the sweet-and-sour
beads of colostrum
that disappear, as if an invisible
strand snapped, from around your breasts.

3.

When I wake from the dream
of a wife, the hurt in my neck's
where I can't reach. I've been sleeping
funny, and now a twist in my intake
of breath must spend the day undoing
the way I'm bent when blacked out.
I can see, where glare hits the window

right, the great vein in my neck,
near the shoulder, fork,
before it roots through the chest,
at the heart of my decision.

WINTER LORE

1.
Cars in ice;
overnight, their engines go dark
to our sensibilities, turn like hearts
at the center
of reptilian systems.
December; a.m. The birds flown
long ago. December; Chicago;
a.m. Stepping in the month's first snow,
I've never been more aware
of the coppery taste
in the blood looping either foot;
a corpuscle brushes against the soles
with the regular beat of a hamster in a wheel
running to keep from frost;
and on that charge alone
do I generate.

2.
The line between the lips thins,
hums a high electrical mmm
to push a tire from slush
or shovel a way
of walking into the world;
gets thinner;
flaps
in the featureless landscape of face;
makes the fading M of a birdshape
we watched disappear through September.

8

TIDINGS

On the beach, under the farthest inch
of high tide, rocks break
at the light tapping touch of water
asking, every night, for admittance.

This is not the sharp break of friends
splitting bread for breakfast, its doughy
geyser rising from the table.
"A drink: to friendship!" But this water,

its dissolution of rock, its nightly knock
against granite, is work
over generations of human bonds.
This rock of a door will never crack

open for the ocean's ransack; only
atom by atom lets go of this
ultimate vestige of the shore
as a sleepwalker lets go

the doorknob, and loses himself to the night.
This rock will only turn to sand
set in the world like a raw pane of glass,
clear, but unshattered, the sea
will only look in through that transparency.

And I have been walking toward this since breakfast.
Dollar bills, broken for change, gleam
in their copper scatter like starfish. These
pennies grow arms. They throw confetti.

Small birds, seagulls and nighthawks, fall
with the splat of beer bottles on the pier
as if christening, as if bon voyage. And
flaming against the flat black, with passengers,

like enormous transoceanic dirigibles,
promises break in the sky.

THE CLASS OF 65

This is how it happens: a man falls
into a trap and becomes a lion. A girl
slips her finger into the sun's revolution,
marries God. Destined surgeons and physicists
are ambushed in the dark mouth
of a guitar. A girl impales herself
on a husband, or The Year's Top Rookie
accidentally defines his future one night
in a waitress's belly.
When a man falls into a trap
he growls, there's no way out, and nothing
to say about it or do but stare up
at the broken lengths of camouflaged flooring
and pace, if they hold up, on all fours.

*

And some of us remain, each New Year's Eve
drink from the same cup, make a frieze
of touching lips around its rim. It's strange
how a word tacked on a doorway pulled me in
a poem for keeps, how you're
in the hands of children, how you're lost searching
for something to spit your heart on
hypodermically thin, and you,
and you, and anyway
our conversation, one shade darker
than empty air, fits in each other's ears
like a cast of the entrance
to our memories; and our presence

is the very space it occupies, we're
that involved. And still,
in the middle of a rebuttal or where a joke
slips off the edge of the visible spectrum,
the mind can click
on something outside that window between two sentences,
and my consciousness ride
hundreds of miles away transfixed
on the red belly-light of an airliner.

*

They're happy to see you. You could be
the guest of honor. Or you are,
your voice is perforated on the microphone.
And such applause!
They could share you all night, the main course,
or, if there's not enough, the skeleton
for the soup pots, or if you can't go around
as a broth, just a light sweat
coating a roomful of foreheads. Don't
begrudge them this or ask
whose animal's trapped and rendered tonight.
You love them, they love you,
and warmly turn over
your hand in their hands,
the lump of soap.

THROUGH THE STATE

The stars we haven't seen in months,
so tenuous. The least imbalance blanks
them out, and either we travel by cloud-cover
or, like crazed horses, over sudden stiles
of searchlights; either way's too much
for something so far from our lives

as guiding configurations. Often I move
by the sound of a rag-shod foot slopped
out of shin-high mud, and know the man
before me's moved a step; the sound of leather
boots in mud is lower, you mightn't know,
but I know, having once misled myself

a mile by following the footfalls of an Officer
through night, and if he'd turned I'd be
roped in a Chevy trunk for sure, the lightbulb
greased and prodded up my rectum
purposely smashed—I've heard such tales;
but by his cigarette I saw the talon-emblem'ed

visor, and stood still; a lizard crawled
my thigh, a scaly mudwen, and pricked a rash
from crotch to shoulder, and still no flinch
betrayed me; now you bet I'm deft, distinguish
cleated heels from naked soles! This week
the proverbial ray of hope: following the refugee

ahead of me in line by the evanescent
braille his stubbled cheek makes pressed
in sleep to the mudflats, I saw
what might be the horizon glow
a line of stars across my vision, auguring
well. Or is that barbed wire?

It's too dark to tell.

PEOPLE ARE DROPPING OUT OF OUR LIVES

Joplin's voice, edged like a crack
in glass, breaks
out from the window and falls
two floors to the cold
campus night.
Across the empty street
one man stopped mid-step
listens attentively in the dim
verge of my peripheral vision.
Nameless, face
half-shadowed and form hunched
anonymous under windbreaker, he
and I balance
our sides of a city block.
Tenuous relationship.
We breathe, we form a spatial border.
In space we define, shape shifts
foot to foot and pocket to pocket.
As he exhales
a long black line of night
plumbs my throat for its measure.

Song:
hemorrhages up over Joplin's lips
and hits curbing. Litter:
cans, packs, crumpled cups
accept her flow and fill
beneath our footfalls like flasks
of invisible blood
from dead friends and lost lovers.
People are dropping out of our lives.

17

Pieces of constellation are missing.
And now, this man,
at his disappearance back
into flat shadow, now
as lamplight and real estate realign
to compensate for his physical absence,
now in that hole
attracting me across the street,
Joplin's words—like coal
never made it to diamond—
smoke the saffron-and-red-hot West Coast blues
from a black metallic brazier.

Nobody near. The house at my back,
my house, is all stoop and sill, all
exit. All panes have a shatter-pitch.
Nobody near. And only the rapid
passing flasher suddenly shines
fingerprints onto my blank window.
By that second of whorls, I know them,
angels of the night.
And, nobody near, and Linda playing
up and down my spine with her ghost hands,
I sing
past midnight with the choir:
Jimi Hendrix, Brian Jones, Jim Morrison,
and Janis. We sing,
the streets don't know what to do with it,
Linda's hands know all the notes,
a high one, a rising falsetto, the scales
tip in the sky and go for broke,
the star, the guitar, the shrieks
go higher, the hands go
capo up my neck.

WARNING THE CROWD

December's between the bricks. You step,
you make ice out of snow. You shout, you
steam. For every action there's an equal
white expenditure. The need to breathe hangs
visibly over the mouth, your oxygen mask,
white cone, your lungs shot
through a bullhorn. Picture the bricks gone
carefully, square by square: the skeletal

frost still stands, or could, an igloo's
blueprint. Picture the crowd: encrusted
in snow like the lost-wax process. Say
no, chafe cheeks, maybe this is the winter
to slit our wrists; not for suicide
—this time for two bones we need
to rub to fire. Say anything they'll applaud
blood to their hands for. Tell them December's

climbing the ice-rungs inbetween bricks,
will reach the roof soon, aim, and pack
his snowballs each around a bullethole.
Tell them run like water. It's in the snow.

AGAINST THE ODOR

Every six seconds the blink lies
to the fovea. The sunspot burns
a hole in the long, looped radio wave.
A dozen roses is eleven
flowers and one mauve chameleon
straining to stamen its tongue. These
be the natural hypocrisies.
In the land of the lie you're shown this

photo: a man standing spreadlegged
"in two states at once!" castrated
by their common edge; the ten inner intervening
tips of a husband's gloves insulate his caress;
and one Jew, thrown to the showers, lifts
the soap to his nose against the odor
of gas, and smells his niece's breast.
The white lie is the nephew

to euthanasia. This is the lie: the worm
in the history text; the alligator purse;
the Catholic virgin saving space in her womb
for eschatology. This is the difficult
rectification: the purse snapped open,
its pink mouse saved from drowning
in the digestive fluids. Keep him whole.
In the land of the lie the one-eyed man

blinks every three seconds. This is the myth
of the land of the lie: that the lamb led
by its tear ducts sees the blade

as just the Utah border. This is the queen
of the land of the lie: whose tongue crawls
into the vegetable bins and ballot boxes
to spread its wet; whose belly is ectopic;
whose menstruation, trompe l'oeil.

SELF-PROTECTION

The shotgun or the coronary: 'll getcha
either way. For instance a girl embodies
a bullet one night on Chicago's South Side
and we're scared, again this season, of anything
with fingers. Any blinking copcar or ambulance
passing by after dark makes a coffin-

suddenly-crowbarred-open-to-flashbulbs
out of our livingroom, for an instant
at least, and we're shot by that glare
from somewhere for a morgueman's file: we know it.
We stay indoors. Our neighborhoods
want to secede, mint their own coins

with toothmarks worried onto spoons
for currency, finally the glass in our windows
bleats against us in bed, wants to snuggle
closer, into and through the pores, make
a delicate cat's-cradle webbing our innards.
Self-protection; and, farther

than finally, we shrivel down to a thumb-sized beast
in the heart, and pace like a zoo wolf there: no wonder,
a rut worn lifelong where it counts, we implode
in the chest in the face of attack.

BECOMING LANDSCAPE

Watching the lake from morning on
you think you'll fall in if you don't clutch a button

or pen cap in your pocket
for life, plug four white nubs of palm

up into the buttonholes. Stand there awhile;
a whine in either ear, for balance.

It takes a day for the sun to burn
your silhouette out from the flat matte background,

right heel up around the head down to left heel.
Don't move; night's a black tuning fork

one prong per nostril;
shiver with it.

Stare at the moon and it's two moons,
left eye and right eye: coins

on your eyes. Stare at them. Now
there's only this, two quarters lost on the beach.

A gull exists twice, once in each pupil,
exactly for the width of each pupil.

The lake washes into your head, washes out.
Only that, a stare like a cove

beyond the need to follow movement,
and two feet silent in sand long after

the fingers kneel, a male and female
quadruped blanking out in the dark.

INTERCOURSE IN BAD WEATHER

Words in transit warp with the cold.
Your voice sieved through the receiver's
seven holes hits my ear as a newspaper photo
reassembles your face for my ear: there's more
of you lost in-between the dots than rides them.
A smile hooks like a horse-shoe

on a telephone pole, its spat word speeding
onward through the wire, or a nuance uses
itself up mid-way to my house in shooting
juice through a bird: some hobo lifting his supper
from a snowbank pries your tongue
from its beak. And here I'm guessing your cunt,

eyes, nostrils, mouth, and ass are each which
of the phone's seven holes; or trying to translate
the ancient language of misinterpretation.
Better to open the door, step over the newspaper
that's my bottom stoop, and follow the wire
back through those neighborhoods words are bruised

and bloodied in. To go's no breeze; when I dialed
the weather lady, her taped voice said *flow snurries
by late*. It's a cold trudge through that.

THE ALWAYS

Lifting the beer, the cup's rusted bottom
falls out, your reflection clinging for life.
The bolts burn brown in all eight corners,
secret ingots: oxidized. Its crack creaked
open enough around the rasping air, the mailbox
says "corrode," speaks in direct address,
it's got your number, your number's up.
This is the shack where a man stops.

This is the county line, these are the hens
dibbling earth whose future is pillows
in geriatric clinics, here are the unmarked unmilked
cows whose future is empty wallets, somewhere
cocoons are lapsing, atom by atom, into wings;
candles are going up in smoke; weeks mildew, outdated.
This is the village where a man stops
for the time to write, for all time

forthcoming to read, to pour his heart out.
But the pump doesn't work. The window's stuck
or broken: there's no halfway here. To catapult
up, meditate in mid-air, and land precisely
at start is the dream belying orbiting,
friction, male menopause. It's in this shack
a man learns what his pencil knew before him:
When time stands still the always

turning world grinds against it.

POEM

Linda, when I write of your name
written on a tree I mean scars
heal. Under years of wood,
the center of an oak is whispering
Linda Linda to itself.
The old philosopher's question: If

nobody hears a tree fall, does it
shout someone's name at its last
emotional moment above-ground?
Ears placed to my chest have heard
welts imbedded inches in
my muscles make a noise of fading

initials, as if poems were disappearing
ink, no more than that, or names
no more than sound waves. Logic
like that says a redwood is nothing
but an unused potential for calendars;
the deeper in, the blanker the dates.

Dear Reader, you are like the poem
I wrote and nailed to a tree
for passersby but the wind
took it, and now
where are you, and I
hardly know your name anymore.

SONG FOR LONGING
—everyone without someone tonight is invited to join in—

Now you will join your tongue with mine.
Now we will be a braid of tongues.
Now anybody who can't reach far
enough on his own, plait tongues with me.
The Eskimaux have twenty names for snow.

Come knot your tongue with me.
Two tongues shall be a lariat.
Three tongues could be a grappling-hook.
The Eskimaux have a hundred names for snow.
A map: four tongues, four ways.

Hold your tongue in your hand, like me.
The Eskimaux have five hundred names for snow.
Point to the Eskimaux. Point north,
how far can one tongue go?
Unroot your tongue from your mouth, like me.

Now our tongues click against our palms
like geiger counters. And now they go
dry in our fingers, and now they know
what word it is that snow says
to the dowsing rod. The Eskimaux

have five hundred names for snow.
The lovers have five hundred names
apiece for Cock and Cunt. The mad
have five hundred names for inexpression,
all unexpressed. It's where we grow

we learn the language. Come throw
your tongue at the window with me.
Come sing your name at that pitch.
Come to my room, break the windows
with me. If I knew five hundred

names, I'd call it a day.
I'd make it a day. I'd call it
The-beginning-of-my-week. It's true.
If once in my life I could unsew
the seam of one tongue, undo the bow

in the mouth of just one other person,
and learn the name inside so well
I could take it in my mouth like snow
against the pain . . . Come, throw
your tongue to the world's tongues

with me. Come to my room,
you should see. Nothing could fill it.
From window to window the space
is so huge, the longing of all
the mad and all the lovers could blow

like a north wind, like a winter wind,
and not be long enough. No breath
could cross a space like that.
No name could ever travel as far as that.
The cold could never drop so low.

The concept of name would never occur
to a man alone in a room. Five hundred
names could be a language, though.
Come to my room, until our tongues turn blue
on the words of the Eskimaux. No matter what

we weather, we'll know where we are, and who.

DUTY

The automatic completion of role: as if
to say by perfectly filling this constriction,
your throat goes numb to the tie's tight grip.

Sometimes the knot in the gut is so great,
the man your size who lives in you
is kneeling in pain with his steel knees

focusing all his hurt weight on your belly.
And what keeps you standing at such a time
if not his position, and your straight windpipe

the only escape for his howling
prayer to heaven? Church
is defined by people bent in two

who are given two choices: death
or walking out. The church itself is busy
admitting sun at a proper slant

through the red-stained glass
and providing a functional space for emotion.
When your father dies there's nothing left

to do but walk in, and comfort your mother.

THE BRITISH IN AFRICA

". . . formula, ritual
saved them"

Black coffee beats at the heart of a day
at your life's most desperate: and two lumps say
all you need to know about how much
sweetness will carry you through to nightfall.
And enter, and face what you must, and shaking
hands with the undertaker, you think of tea served

daily at 4 in the china cup on a magistrate's mid-jungle
verandah, something out of a Joyce Cary novel you read
ten years ago; and you realize every hand shook
sitting *shiva* acts as a momentary rung
up a terrible rockface. And when you wake
alone in bed for the first time, the first thing

you do's brew a pot. Now, somewhere, darkness
shadows an unmapped veldt ravine, and cold wind cuts
through muscle as through a strawman's chest,
a chasm where some man could lay his blueing cheek
on the bottom brush and gibber and sleep lost
even to air-search in such unruly tangle. But you

grip safe to doorknobs, faucets, and dress
like the British in your own version of formal whites;
a new day's undershorts, catching you, this
net above where the drop is deepest.

THE ONLY POEM,
FOR HANNAH SPIVACK AND PAUL CARROLL

Phlegm, piss, shit, sweat: oh we know
how to name the glues. My aunt had tubes
up her nose for the oxygen, and my uncle wept,

he'd been saving two tears
like a marble Madonna. Well I don't want to know
what it takes to make igneous rock or crockery

saline; enough, I won't say a hard-on is bagged
bleeding, the tail of the sperm
a lash. There are kinder visions: a hen

can aim an egg through her cloaca, she won't miss,
it won't break. There are things
of beauty: I'm going out to water the backlawn flowers

if my zipper unsticks. And I'll take them
by the dozen to my aunt, she's bringing it up now
thick as a porridge. The nurse had to watch

all night. Okay, yes, so we have to face it.
It's night: a hen
folds like a tendon. We're all in neat bundles

for processing. The only dream's
of the orderly's flashlight, my aunt whose liver
heaves like a leech, and a teacher-poet

who told me, once, his tongue
dunked in the seventh beer: Albert,
there are only three lines:

one of the brain, one of the prick, one of the heart.
There is only one poem,
and this is its tercet.

HOW TO KEEP WARM IN FEBRUARY

The origin of the valentine: 14th century England
women menstruating with sexual passion;
as secret sign to their lovers, this red heart
shaped card: "it bleeds for thee." Oh vaginal
lore and legends! that the hymen of our half-beast
female ancestry blinked like an eyelid, thus
that women still wink their eyes while flirting,
thus Cupid works by dark and his farflung arrows
prick when "love is blind"; that whale-pussy,
water-tight else the female whale would drown
her young, hauled humankind as hull of the first ship
crossing sea from Asia to New World, the men
supposedly so worn by a month-long sojourn
in such depths, the colony perished: no new generation;
that lady police place cameras there, identifying rapists;
that Siamese women have one for each twin; or white
women, two for segregation; that in the ancient myth
world of love, the cunt and the mouth once interchangeable:
thus, fellatio now as the unbalanced half of a time
when ladies spoke, and honestly, through the vagina:
thus that the tongue fits perfectly; that the "cross
bones" can catch a man in there and keep him surely
or more surely than that same man's finger slipped in
a marriage ring; that "cross bones" may be a lie;
still all men have been stuck there once and most
forever; that girl over there, alone, her matchstick
polio legs: though they be thin, at the pulse-point
where they meet could flame; that I ask her name;
that the strike come quickly.

DEATH AND RESURRECTION THROUGH GLASS

Mirror-glass as momentary death-mask: pressed,
a sudden thickened air, on the tinfoily face. It's
chilling, a thought like that, your casual moue
above the bedroom dresser become a cadaver's stare,
it makes a personal winter for you in the middle
of Chicago's winter. Look, it's freezing, your breath frosts

fronds, December lacework, over your look
out a window. Maybe you shiver at that
white parody of Spring, those exhaled ferns existing
without regard for chlorophyll; or maybe
you take hope, remembering
breath-fogged glass as sign

the lips aren't quite a corpse's yet. If so,
a faith in cycles implies the time
the rainpipe's cram will thaw, and poems
buried on the desktop rustle.
The winter town in the glass
paperweight: has to be turned on its back

like any ice-skinned stick-limbed sparrow caught
unsheltered by the killer cold, before
the world is righted, snow finally falls, and birds
are reported returning, punctually from the south.

CONVERSION

Myths of its melting, of sinking through it like cloudbanks
aside, the snowflake's edge is jagged. It's a deadman's
Star of David, six straight lines connected by soldering
frozen spit at the corners, here comes the rabbi of snow
with his white coat buttoned up by stones and coal-black
eyes fresh from the oven. He'll convert you, yes

you'll don the scarf and gloves of the sect, its secret
signs: the nerves dead up the cheeks, the puckered nipples.
And he'll give you this *mezuzah*, this symbolic flake hung
silver at the chest. And when in March it's almost melted
it whispers myths of rebirth, and you'll bend to hear it better,
bring the sixth sharp side your lambswool-coddled throat, for Spring,

your offering.

JAN. 31

1.

For rings and anklets
they hacked off
just below the knee or the elbow
on the female corpses; the male captives
witnessed this, their eyelids
razored off, and then were thrown
beneath the axe four times themselves
to taunt the streetdogs
at the Babylonian marketplace
with a highflung arm or leg; the pups
would lick the stumps on the stiller bodies.
Everyone loved this; there, the peddler
hawking balls of sweetmeat at the scene
of a river eel fed hand over hand
up the vulva, or of leather wet
and tied around the testicles to dry, he lost
an eye himself in the wars once and, they say,
would earn full twice what he now gets
for his spiced strips of pork-fat
if not for the foreigners
herding their own plump swine so close to the border.
And the King?: undoes his plait of hair
and comes to his favorite concubine
with a gift tonight, this bead-fringed crotch-piece
of fleece and human eyelids.
*
And this: because
of one wet-nurse
whose milk has dried, whose teeth have gone,

whose begging-bowl at the temple gate is full
with ants again this evening, and who
in all this sleeping town is the only one to pray
the men of Sumer and Akkad leave the garrisons
moan in the wind
and return to the cowsheds and millet-plots;
this: because she prays to Ea,
god of waters, he of life-wet
flowing from his body, Father Ea
Whose Wisdom Is Infinite
for wells are deep and streams
devious, who from the whole
Babylonian pantheon alone
invariably protects and advises
humankind, whose ablution-house
is rain itself, great goat-fish god
who dies and is nightly reborn, resplendent, in Ocean; this:
a poem for the astronomer
who fixed Ea in the sky.
*
I picture him
pinpricking stellar maps
in a moistened clay ephemeris
from a ziggurat's top
150 feet
above where the last of the sacrificial blood
stains the altars. It's chilly,
just a bit, but he's still and the cloak about him
assumes the semi-permanence of a tent
to stand till morning. Another star:
another prick. The headband's knotted
above his eyes to show how past and future
knowledge meet here, strengthen his gaze.
Another prick: another locus

of a god. His father's father mapped the moon
appear each night against a further astral pattern
in the annual circling of sky. And now,
this man, another dot, his looking
up to where events on earth are foreordained
in counterparts of light, he charts another line
in the body of stars
that appears to men, inevitably,
as a Water Bearer.
In Babylon it was Ea.
In ancient Egypt, Khnum.
In Greece, Ganymede.
*
In America it's winter.

2.
We're cold.
In January the wind could gibber
so through any conch, through any ear,
the lake would freeze
down to the rooted ovum in its bottom-most bass,
or the pineal gland
in a human brain mistake itself
for a hailstone. We're cold, beware
the polar bear. Here anything
could freeze, each onanism
is a tiny glittering
grapnel in the room; the very air goes rigid, blinking
scratches clawmarks
on the evening's tightened surface, and we take this
for a sign: beware the polar bear.
We're cold. We're clinking.
Winter is acquisitive: it wants the spit

between the teeth, the moist breath of the armpit;
we can watch the spread of frost,
an arctic fungus, up the lengths of us. The polar bear?:
watch out, it's reached the city limits.
Speech: a whitened cud, a pellet of ice
to cluck beneath the tongue, fellatio
with the teakettle has no ameliorating effect.
We're cold. We're chattering. The uvula
hangs iced, the penis in its marital glove
still shivers, nothing helps, the nipples contract,
lactation needs a hole
chipped with a hatchet. This is January:
sausages of ice in the bowels, and wind so quick
its edge could strop your neck
and the traitor-flesh
rise to meet it, wind so sharp
it makes an acupuncture through the pores,
a winter wind: a coup de grace. A heave of snow
in such a wind: the landscape's
white grand mal. We're cold, it's winter,
nothing helps, and all we can do in wariness
is watch the season's steady blanch
for the death-bear's nose, its small brown
rectal star; for its teeth
are at one with the weather.
          *
Or:
can something help? Can this machine
compressing twelve months' news to logs?
Combatting winter: could our love,
could friction, keep us warm? Perhaps
if we undo our scarves and sip
a fizzing champagne from your one good galosh . . .
combatting cold.

And snuggling
beneath the electric blanket, plugged in
to each other . . . isn't this
the long-sought antidote? But
in the darkness, one deep coil vibrates
with affinity for police receivers, picks up
this night's news: there are miles of fire hose
gone solid as locomotive rails
with ice, there's an infant
perfectly preserved after thirty days
in the pond, there are cars even now
beginning to slide
no matter what we press on; and
in the January night we wake,
our chests
beneath the chilling weight
of a blanket
radioing for help.

3.
And you say I'm cold
in mid-May, I'm the snowman,
no heart, words drop from my mouth
like lumps of coal. You say a woman could
go snowblind hunting veins
that work in a mind like mine,
that tic or run, you pity
all the girls who left my bed
frostbitten, picture a pile of blue,
amputated breasts. Not true. Last night
while you slept miles away, contentedly,
your body's primal she-beast
drugged, and senseless to its estrus: I

was turning on the mattress in a sweat than stank,
a roast shank.

*

A broken record's the lullaby
insomnia taps its foot to.
There's an endless song, a small baton
to shake like a thermometer; a small
piano keyboard, smaller, maybe
it's a book of matches. Heat
strikes up a tune. The foot won't fall asleep.
It's manic. Now it dances
out from under the leg,
on fire, scarfed in ashes. Well,
it's not a happy fever and a song sung long enough's
a tongue in spasm; so I play my life:
eye as turntable, pupil
spindled with lamplight, night a needle
scratched again and again through the brain's thin grooves.
It's hot; and when it's this hot
you sink easily through linen, you're the soup
your own bones float in, here's your soul,
it's little more than seepage.
There's an endless song: you're something
that's spilled. There's a small piano:
you're dampness. A man could fall to his nerves
like a man in a net,
it almost gives at his weight,
a man could hang above the sore
that's buried in the mattress. There's a wink:
eight hours; a swallow: all night.
A man remembers more regrets
than numbers. Here, your life, the tune:
you're nothing more than salt water
and the bed screams

when you reach its wound.

*

It's not a happy fever. But
it's heat, and sometimes needed. Ea
in Hellenistic Greece became *Oannes,*
and later, in Christendom,
John, "John, John, da Baptist man,
dipped 'em in an' out again."
To spend a night with nothing
but your errors at your side, is an oblation
to the Babylonian sky, is to be baptized
in the thick sweat
of repentance. Love,
another morning; call me: SU 4–6882.
The SU's Sunnyside. It's true. In the middle
of all that chills, at the silver pulse of the snowflake,
a man can kindle an atom of warmth
to keep his thinking
heliocentric, a block of ice
and its potential for thawing
are one, to melt's
to turn to spirit.

*

"Our blood
in fact has a chemical composition analagous
to that of the sea of our origins. The sea
where living creatures were at one time immersed
is now enclosed within their bodies." Somehow
I never doubted it. Stars
seen through this blizzard mark the month: I walk,
a he-beast
in its rut, to where they're clearest. On the beach
a lone fish-skeleton filled with snow
becomes a symbol of patience. Sun:

45

the snow between the scales glares. January the 31st.
*

This frost, this ice,
these water bearers.

4.
History repeats itself.
Two boozing Babylonian soldiers slouched
against a mud-brick wall for shade at mid-day
pit the teeth in a booty-pouch,
about to refine the sister arts
of gambling and deception. Here,
these loaded dice, this mouth of mine
designed to splat in a corner and roll up
losers every time, spits out the pocked words
of a poem again. This clear false-bottom
shot-glass, never
holds the gulp you need: my voice . . .
What does it matter? A few more days
and the King will die, and these two soldiers,
part of a retinue of guards and serving girls
that numbers up to seventy, will look up
from the pit-bottom
where they flank the royal tomb, then willingly
—all of them, sentinels, harp-maids,
ox-grooms—dip their cups in the proffered bowl
and lie down in neat rows, no peg
or head-dress plume misplaced, before
the poison hits completely. After the oxen
are slaughtered, the dirt's filled in.
*

A winter morning; I can see
my upper lip (its crow-in-flight outline

and network of cracks)
done up in grease,
as in lithography, push off
from the china rim
across the coffee's steaming surface.
Once, it flaps; then warps; then disappears.
A death,
no matter how small, makes a small constellation.
The long stem of urine,
the yellow bloom in the bowl . . . There is
no detritus, no scab, no snakeskin
that doesn't partake of the luminous effluvium
of rotting. Norman Morrison
Gone Up In Smoke, Monroe's Red Lips,
Great Falstaff Rising. Once and for all:
there are mythicizing patterns . . . here,
the shape sun picks
in these dust motes . . . remember?
*
A court astronomer dies; and is buried
appropriately, with the funerary urns
of his signs and stations, under the temple
near the ziggurat complex.
The man who fixed Ea in the sky
is placed in earth; three billion cells
each sixty seconds in a living human being . . . maybe,
isn't it true, we die
into what we cherished? And a constellation,
newly-born, swings out of the hilled horizon,
The Astronomer Ascending. Or not
a congery of stars perhaps, but a single star
to shed the light
a poem like this is read by. Or,
no star, but in your eye,

right now, a glimmer of light
the size of a pen-point
to burst in appreciation.

*

He squared Apsu's quarter, the abode of Nudimmud,
The Great Abode, Esharra, which he made as the firmament.
Anu, Enlil, and Ea he made occupy their places,
He constructed zones for the gods of the months.
After the water of creation had been decreed,
After the name "abundance" born in heaven,
The lord of the abyss, Father Ea,
Built his sea-house of silver and lapis lazuli.
Its silver and lapis lazuli, like sparkling light,
The father fashioned fittingly in the abyss, praise Ea.

*

Space curves
and returns upon itself. This is fact.
If vision were absolute, if I could look
that far, I'd see a man
with pen bent over a page
of cheap blue-ruled three-ring school notebook paper
writing this. To enter
January, smack
at twelve on New Year's Eve, and tremble
with the contact of your sole on snow,
a moment only, as if
the circular year were knotting
its past and future ends
in you . . . Isn't the zodiac
a ring . . . or what I want to say
is a headband
knotted on a Babylonian brow.
It's winter, the wind hits hard,
your skin went long ago

but you can feel the brain
bunch between your eyes.

5.   *1973*

Winter is the real drought. Whatever trickled, once,
now's a blunt instrument. We're lame, we're lean.

This is the week of The Honorable Peace, and today,
today's my birthday. At midnight

I walked under trees until a star like light
flecked on a focusing eyeball stared

through the oval touch of two branches,
and wanted to tell me something

about a losing and gaining of years. I think
of all the others, in Egypt, in Ur,

who were also buried
along in the unescapable overhanging of earth

when a ruler died. The political life . . .
how it wants the wrists and ankles! Now,

to be 25, and to trust
in the ancient myths of cycle and rebirth,

their small, sentimental proof: one tear
under Aquarius.

MARRIED IN THE PRESENCE OF THE LORD

1.

Negative proof, as in: you believe
her faithful, and she does nothing
to disprove you. You do not romp
like a puppy and bark "here! this
clinches it!" at the rise of a specific
volcano in your life, but the two
of you merely grow old together
with your hands entwined
around the little negative space
you share when the palms meet.
Of course, the dog you jointly own
makes a mess of things, but cleaning
up together you say "if it don't shit
sometimes, it ain't living."

2.

Thus to give her the opportunity
of negative proof, give opportunity.
Men wink, flex, thumb rides
and checkbooks. But you believe
in her. It is religion
not when God signs the bill
in fire across the cirrus sky but
when God doesn't, and in the still
air still the pious accept Him.
So on any given day there is no thunder
in the faucet, ocher earthquake clattering
under the cup, or any chattering messenger
birds from far lands, but just the dumb dog yelps
like crazy at the door when she comes back.

KARTOON KAPERS

1.

Clear winter night; crack ice and a mile of air
cracks with that sound. Your breath is a loaf.
You could carry it home. First,
starlight drilling amber lamplight,
you shuffle in front of the countless edges
snowfall breaks light on, and find your year's
first joy in the radiance glittered out at your life
from a frosted bench-leg. In the alley
a mouse hands a cat a stick of dynamite.

2.

Suppose my pores fell off
and tinkled like a spilt moneybag
on the bike path—I was about
to write that;
but realized how the pores are entrances
long breath-tunnels
wind from in a maze
through the meat and the wet of the body.

3.

A steam-shovel closes its maw
around a badguy, chews, spits
out the bones.
Suppose a hammer-whacked thumb grew
to the size and hue of a ripe tomato;
a tree tugged its roots up to sashay
to Bach; a man walked away
from a boxing glove with his pupils
spinning their sockets like roulette balls;

the cow gave chocolate milk; a woman
steps off a ten-story ledge and doesn't fall
till she looks down; it's 1958, this happens
often: suddenly, reddening skies, a cigar
explodes in a cop's piss-frightened face
with all the destructive force
of a charred banana; or, no, it's a duck
who steps off the ledge and falls shrieking.

4.
Or, maybe, suppose
a man drops to his knees in snow
with all the weight from his knees up
pressing him flat against a ground
that's less than zero.
Suppose a pain like that. A gray pain.

5.
Or suppose such pain never happened
and, you felt, caught in the interplay of stars
and iceshine, never might; and
you could tramp home through snowpowder
smiling
truer than a steam-shovel with a face
could ever break into grins.

PACT

"Goose-bumps": capillaries constricted, blood warmth
conserving itself, one layer down, against the chill.
Bad enough, and heat hangs in your breast like beef
in an ice-lined boxcar. Best for your climate to reach,
and include, your perimeter; think of the line sea
evaporates up from, and air churns into foam down through,

when you're in a woman; somewhere's a speck that's sperm
and ova equally, overlapped interstices, and it bobs
in both your boilings. Think of ejaculation as penning
a peace treaty on your common border, a promise inviolate
states will share fuel, should one come close to freezing.
And, muffed safe in sex, you're sorry you ever plucked

anything tuftless, and wonder what of your sweats
and oils soaking into the pillow it takes to fat
those feathers for flight again; and dream that
would be your pact with Nature, a goose you saw
coasting the nation once: brilliant quill on quill
on quill, and each pointing heartward, its hidden tip

signing a name on the line, in blood.

WATER PIE: TONIGHT, 12/11/72

Tonight the air's too dry, the vents
offsetting winter cold with the enthusiasm
of retrorockets, until we're dry-mouthed
at the blast and the rims of our nostrils
cake. And in defense we scatter water

filled pie tins through the house;
in sleep, the nose sniffs in a wedge
of water pie, as much as, or more
than, the dog laps at night. Tonight,
when I wake you, my lips burn to lick

your silhouette so that it gleams in moonlight
like halved citrus, want to stop to suck
a flower of blood to your chillest hill
this season, but then continue and touch
you with my expenditure

of this wet as uniformly as it was breathed in.
There's just enough left, a circle
in the aluminum pan, to catch the arid
moon as if it snuck to drink from a gleaming
trap at our bedside. I've no sense,

it seems, of decorum; tonight there are men
on the moon. Well, let them look
down at us if they'd like! We're all
busy, reaching as far as we can,
and perhaps this makes us brothers. I know

when I walk the dog this morning he'll piss
at every tree on the block, his way of claiming
territory with water he's taken in, no pee
in the world smelling just like his. It's
a home. And I sight the sun through his flags,

his warm waves of stink on the cold wind.

SONG FOR PURE DIRECTION

You wanted your life to show direction,
some inexorable traversing, the motion
in phloem, the path up the vulva,
the space through which nib points
to page. You wanted your poem's goal
defined: the noon sun silhouetting
a fledgling's first migration.
You wanted the poem between fixed points:
the bird's breast; the quill in the inkwell.

You wanted your love to show direction,
the magnetized penis floating in blood,
a formula for empathy times
the number of overlapping lengths
of snake separating cow from rattler.
You wanted to love everyone in County Jail
through her, a woman with seams so sure,
not one wayward drop escaped
the funnel-shape her legs made.

You wanted your body to show direction,
a ribcage to sizzle like rashers
in sunrise, an eye the goose aims
south through, a tip so close to sunset
it warmed with the weed in the cow's
second stomach, the neon dotting the i
in Police, and the egg accumulating
in the sleeping peacock when everything else
petrified under moonlight. Or

you wanted to *be* the direction, not
the compass needle sewing
the forest northward, no, but its stitchwork
split down a sloughed skin; or a tree
one half moss, one half missing.

THE DISASTER TREE

In the land of the blind
the shade of this tree stretches
farther than the eye can see.
Its roots run deeper than mere defoliation

knows; and even diseased and cut
to a stump, the least half-inch left
level on dirt is the base of a magic space
leading the eyes up

the tree the blind see, to where its invisible
birds sing inaudible notes of hope;
its xylem are still cocked toward heaven.
And even when we fall to our knees

the paper-thin skin
covering the patella is a minimal cushion
we mustn't deny, for in retrospect
it suffices. This poem written on the dead

trunk, on paper, is for the deflowered
flower-girl whose boyfriend may yet do her
justice, insurance, legal heirs, and joy;
this poem is for the proposing boyfriend

whose kneel is forced, but who may one day rise
into his wife with a true love, the force
of which needed such a long distance
runner's start; this poem to say the depths

of despair is where the lowest root drinks
underground streams, and continues
past disaster; this,
a love poem; this extended conceit, a note of hope:

the tree surgeon falling limb to limb:
when he lost his eyes, he read bark with his fingers.
And when he sawed off his hand, the stump
of his arm could still point, and beckon, and stroke.

FLUX

The lie of permanence: portraiture
chemically changing before our eyes
and behind the impasto eyes of the portrait.
But this could drive us crazy. Luckily,
everything is relative; our wives or parents
defining stability in a human way
contrasted to weather or galaxy-clusters.
This is one of the joys of marriage.

We are busy contemplating a nipple
swelling, like a red berry, in milk.
What a breakfast! Who could digest
the fleeting thought—or who would want to?—
of burying parents, or bearing progeny,
seen not in terms of pathos or bliss
but as your wife's portrait: the oils
changing in the face, mellowing, combining.

Flux: an empty picture frame
falling through the universe.
As it enters earth's atmosphere it falls
through time. It has done similarly
in conceptual fields of other planets.
This is the only way it ages. One moment
before you are any older it flash
ed past you. But—ah, you were busy.

THE EMPEROR'S NEW CLOTHES

1.

In a farm village near the foothills
everybody gives his all
against the wild dog.
No longer will it stalk dark cobbled ways
and drag a breast
out into the shadowy bramble land
from a nightgown.
Everybody stands close. The little ones
climb up stools to be high enough,
the bed-ridden reach their hands through windows.
This is at dusk, and I've seen it.
And one bulb burns
all night in the square
on lactase. If their hands grip tight,
in summer, I mean no gloves, they can do
a hundred watts. And startling moths
ring around the light
of the gut's breaking down milk sugar.

2.

Caloric expenditure
glows. It can't be seen, cartoons
of a light bulb rising over the gray horizon
thought makes in the skull
are approximation. But take her to bed
and there both be one needle
piercing its own eye. Aren't you blind
then
with radiance? It slips over both your heads
for your nightshirts.

3.
Midnight;
your hands on her breasts;
their warming.
Or see, as if through a rift in sense perception,
the kitchen wall
that faces the cut side
of a halved lemon
gleam. Or peel back the fragrant skin;
to go down, like a mouth,
on the juicer.

4.
Or not the trackless foothills, but my basement;
and no coyote or wolf,
but a sad toy poodle too dumb to give paw.
Could you come with me, at three or four
in the morning, and see his ears' insides,
his petals . . .
There are capillaries to trust
as Edison, tungsten . . .
hydroelectrics
my tongue runs in you.

CAR RADIO

Einstein said the equivalent of rubber
baby buggy bumpers; that's comfort
enough when driving this far this
fast, the women a ten-mile flash

of hemline, the men a hairline busy
advancing and retreating on a blur,
all names one syllable caught
from a mouth zoomed by your looking

out the window, and the cornfield's black
loam spokes forever turning past
your car at a speed exactly
matching yours: comfort enough,

and necessary, to heist a bar of rock
and roll in one neighborhood and sing,
years later in some city where the call letters
spell nothing you recall, the same tune:

prom night, summer '65. The theory:
the quicker the speed the less
you age, the quickest the speed
gets is a perfect immutability.

And this small reassurance, this
stanzaic repetition or chant
of similes that's the hole
the dee-jay pins the record with,

always moves with you: like the tire
rolling a stationary line
by moving circles; like the snatch
of music in your brain polishing

a patch on the skull you could see
your high school sweetheart in;
like a child's nonsense phrase
said over and over and over

and over so fast it loses itself
in the string of its saying, and threads
through your life like something to wind
back up to home, there *is* a relative

immortality to axle speed, yours
the sub-atomic face reflected
in the hubcap's center, still
point the world revolves around.

THE LOST FIRST DECADE

Without a caption one might never know Mickey
for a mouse, the tail and lack of finger
not making him human any less; or, more,
the smile, knowledge of how to gum up
tin cans into a submarine, and faith
in how "the Desperadoes will wind up bee-hind bars!"

make him a better man than I ever grew up into.
I've still the hat: and don't I feel silly now,
a bearded 25, with huge black plastic ears
for a yarmulke. Except I *want* to whistle
on the el as if the whole rush-hour jam would nod
in time on its way to work and easily break

out harps strung from suspenders, drums
from gutted attache cases, or the girl in the corner
blow a ragtime clarion on her prosthetic leg.
There's a thumb in my lover's nipples
I suck. And in the dark, though I've never said it,
haven't I gasped around something, it's Minnie

undoing her blouse for the glass of warm milk.

NOSTALGIA

Childhood: preconstructing the future.
Against The Four Seasons' and The Beach
Boys' static falsetto background,
like a miniature hand-held toy
derringer against an early '60's lakeshore
sky filled solid gray with the invisible
interstices of rock-and-roll, Albert
booms out the cannonball of daydream.

He will this, he will muscle
his clapboard slat ribs Superhero
full, he will that, he will own
his own car and a bordello, he will
such-and-such, he will soforth.
Suddenly there's an interim.
We are never conscious of it until,
like sleep, it is over. Nostalgia

requires this immense and empty stage.
When we reach its lip, we stutter at first
with fright at the other gun
in this poem, way back at the EXIT,
aimed at our spotlighted heads.
But the audience settles elbows
and thighs into indentations comfortable
enough to seem their own, made during,

and waiting since, a previous lakeshore
concert. This is the definition of Home
and everyone is happy. And now by way
of introduction we encapsulate, in the comic
book word-balloon at our mouths,
this poem's first stanza. Introducing Top
Hot Rock, cool cats, the big one, Little
Albert and The Dynamos! Yeah!

THE STORIES

1. *Grown*

They were coming back! the spectacled moles
parading toward his bedroom window, toads
in spats and tartan vests were returning
tonight, he could see them by starlight
gleaming off gold-tipped walking canes.
He'd better pour ale and warm the buns!
if they stayed, the stocking-capped bear cubs,
the wrens in caps, and the rabbits with maps,
and cats with travel bags, and badgers.
He'd better start the cocoa warming!
But then they passed by and when he leapt up
waving, they screamed and fled far
from the beer growing flat and the bread
growing hard and the milk spilt.
There was no use crying. But what had he done
in these last twenty years to upset them so?
to so change them?

2. *Linda's*

When the phone rings, answer.
Only that.
Just say you remember my address.
Say it's the house where the light
is on. Tell me the liquid of my sores
will harden into garnets. Say that every roof
will grow a flag, or every plate hold oatmeal.
In a fairy tale I read once, a duck
hid a fox, a lamb, and a talking
ladder safely in his throat
till the King's men had passed by him.
Talk to me.
I'll believe anything.

WINTER PRAYER

1.

Cold: the absence of heat,
the zero
cinching a house like mine.
Inside, the breaths of sleepers
rise, even-spaced as yawns
notched on a rawhide belt.
Outside, it's cold. Inside,
*
our hip-bones: stropped
by the belt about us.
I wake, my teeth blue cobalt
in their centers, to kick the furnace
hot; and need to write a prayer
to say the belt may tighten
unmercifully, but leather breathes
*
(a fact) all night,
though its skeleton's long frosted-over.

2.

Somewhere
on the bunk bed riveted in
a wine cellar,
one man's brain dissolves
in the roseate air,
leaving only what he already knows

in his head
in the shape of a bramble bush.
*
A girl
on a chaise-lounge inhales
the bubble
her lowering eyelids will press
down the nightmare's
long hypodermic.
This could happen. It does
happen. Somewhere
*
a bone in a sleeping child's leg
goes soft as chalk
or crumbles away
at the knee in the shape
of a rat-bite; or
the battery clicked off between a man's eyes
leaks, vinegary, with disuse; or
in a dormitory
far from here, the bodies are stacked
like geological strata
and a pain wells up
the length of a column of nipples.
*
And, given
I've seen in winter
how the breath diminishes
over distance,
this prayer I say in the mouth
my mouth fidgets
into the pillow
is not for them

*

though they may be right
in the backyard, thinner than the lining
in a coat of snow.

*

This is all I can do:

3.

*everyone
reading this, you're welcome
to sleep in my house; here, anyone
unconscious and hugged
to his linen, his floe
through the turbulent sleep:*

*

*when that sheet's down
to the size of eye-white,
wake to find it's taken you somewhere
serene and back.*

*

*And pray for the coal, not the furnace-coal,
but the eyes in the backyard. For they only read
the absence of all color.*

THE CONCEPT OF VOICE IN FICTION

Imagine making love in an arena.
Around the rim of the pit, the person's
face, set flush against our lustings,
watches. Then, the crackling PA system
would be his mouth reporting to us
everything we do. The pit
would be his eye. We writhe in it.
I am your lover, and I am the first
person, and he is making us

up, to do things for him. Even arm's-length
back from the railing, his lidless eyes
never leave his fiction. He needs us,
vicarious passion, and his distance
far from anything that can pale
or purple is our strength. Let him
see "they did such-and-so" saying
"we" for "they" and "I" for "he"—let him
live in us, if he wants, a fetus

we can try to bring closer.
But also, imagine my entering
you, your own metaphorical arena,
while he keeps screaming "I
love you! I love you!" in places
where I should speak—my mouth,
for instance, your body-holes. Who
am I? the man with his tongue
up your love? or the voyeur

whose gloved tongue is in my tongue
as the author who shaped me, or baby
I could shape, is in me? partaking
of these words. Such are the questions
one of us asks; the answer is: we speak most
truly about ourselves when we call
us by other names. My name
when I open my mouth is the hole
in the condom through which the third person escapes.

HANDICAPS

The poet in the prince
in the frog in the storybook:
surely whoever bothered with him
under all that, would
truly love him. The princess, too,

kept kosher: couldn't eat
Chinese food or leave the castle
until Sabbath's sun set—a drag
to date. Who would want to
finish such a fairy tale?

except a connoisseur of such.
So this is precisely the point
my beard makes
an inch below my chin: how
frisked, unhired, suspect,

it leads my head smack
dab toward the one kiss
sure to make me leap
out of the lily-pond.
It's a lonely plot, but a happy

climax: wedding, bedding, life
long warmth. When the court
salesman tries to sell them family
insurance, the royal couple beg
him to leave: "Handicaps

be insurance of success
enough." Even this poem,
bogged frogpond-deep down
in flimflam: insures I love you
who persevere to the last

stanza: in which the joyous
couple keep kosher, refuse
the fete of frog's legs, remembering,
and having hope for, those
legless, the lame, the yet-unloved.

LETTER TO FRIENDS EAST AND WEST

What's new? I'm still in Illinois,
and the pamphlet says I can find white squirrels
in Olney if I wait long enough. They're rare
you know, and a dung-daubed boy from Kinderhook
swears how their whiskers are each attuned to one
of the four Primeval Whites: snow,
milk, sperm, moonlight, but that's just a rumor;
the squirrels are fact. And there's a gorge "nearly
200 feet deep" near Starved Rock; if it's no
Grand Canyon, Diane, if cracks don't zag here
quite like they do near the nation's extremes,
your awesome schisms, still even *my* disappointments
won't fill 200 feet though I chunk them like stones
all day at the face in the crick at bottom. All night
a wind howls through, and scours out Skeleton
Cave, The Giant's Bath Tub, Well-In-The-Wall
and hones the Illinois rock: Twin Sisters, cradled,
Needle's Eye, pierced, The Devil's Smokestack, pared and polished,
you'd have to see such wind to understand
what shaped the raking hands
above my sleep, you'd have to let it
sodomize you too or hear it lap once
at your mattress. It's not easy here, white squirrels
are never easy. I wouldn't lie to you. But
Abraham Lincoln christened the town of Lincoln,
Illinois by squeezing a watermelon onto the dust
and it's hard, as you could intuit, to run from a state with stains
like that; and even you, as far as Maine or Florida, will think
of that story the next time a sweet rivulet of any kind
froths, rich, across your lips. And didn't you write me,

Ron, to say how deer in California print the Silverado Trail right up
to your sill, you parse out apples, four deer legs are dark
bars squares of sunlight cool in. Well in Illinois we've sows
like troughs of oleo, we've rat-packs in Chicago
till our sewerpipes shake with all the will
of epileptic nerves, and a broom-handle
chopped across the gnawing snout-bones sometimes
does no good. But, though there's nothing so far north
in my life as the bear, so thinking
as the porpoise, here in Illinois is dark
the thickest filament from a sweet corn
couldn't glow through, here's a dark in the field just made
for our own mammalian radiation and, though it's low,
it's light, this star in the Illinois night,
this udder. All I need to do is bide my time:
no kidding, Olney hosts white squirrels
"unique in all the world" and I adopted the stance
of a beech last week to coax them,
wish me luck. The search is difficult, yes, and nothing
even so small as a white incision tooth or whitish pap
as yet rewards my diligence. But, honestly, a plaque
outside of Byron commemorates soldiers under Major Isaiah
Stillman who shot point-blank at a band of Black Hawk Injuns
approaching with the truce flag; you can't just high-tail out
of a land like that, it deserves a certain observation
or, perhaps from the damp underside of the brain,
one root. In any case, Ron, when you visit
bring Cheri, tell me what a twin bed's like, here
"once each year the town of Nauvoo celebrates The Wedding
of Wine and Cheese Festival"; it's true, I'll show you.
I'm in Illinois. I know: a statue of William Jennings Bryan
"created by Gutzon Borglum," I have: trilobites
in the Jersey County quarries, shell bracelets, chert blades
and stemmed stone hoes from the giant Cahokia mounds.

When you were in last May you'd say the ocean
defines *expanse*, report how you chugged up from New Haven, Conn.
to the Cape, there are stories of coeds and jellyfish, Michael,
I believe them all. Now
you must believe me: I'm still here, remember,
Illinois? A man could kneel to Apple River to drink
and let the touch of his tongue go
mainlining, quick, a fix, through the evening prairie;
maybe my mouth gone silver in the rush of the Kaskaskia,
the Sangamon, the Sinnissippi, Big Slough, Vermilion River,
or the Kankakee, is even now a shine at the lip
of far-off faucets, intimacy with me will not sustain
and still: I'm here, I'm pouring, I know, if one is patient
there are white squirrels. I wouldn't bullshit you,
my friends. I'm stuck, half-chance, half-choice, and some
left over to weep in the stand of virgin white pine
along Rock River. Really. Can you imagine? I'm
still in Illinois, I've waited long enough
for anyone else to meet and mate
and raise a whole teat-dangled brood, and still
the Olney Woods has not released its secret beasts
for my catching. Someone . . . Can't you see him,
year after year, running for squirrels like these with the taste
of Devil's Kitchen Lake in his cheeks,
sun on his scalp and dust up his breathing,
screaming through Geneseo
and Bald Knob and Burnt Prairie and Peoria
and Kickapoo "I'm here
I'm here in Illinois with the nation's
oldest evaporated milk plant!"
How could it *not* be true?

A WINTER MINIMAL

I want to be the thankful man
who sucks the pebble to tease
spit from his cheeks, and tastes
how abstinence encircles it
like a fruit. Plant that
kind of pit, and gravel's a kind
of cornucopia; that kind of man,

doesn't need much, says
isn't it true
the hour in my hourglass
has shuffled
between the auricle and ventricle now
for twenty-five years
amen. I've seen that kind of man,

we've seen sun facet lakes in rising,
he's said look how fire survives
in water
by keeping its source in sight.
I want . . . and then
the laying-on-of-hands
known by a dollar bill

in one day: could keep me warm through this season.

HOW WE MET

This year winter lasts late
into April, early night
staining onto the streets from under cars,
over the curbs, up the stoop.
I think of shadows
—how sometimes the light we live by
is measured by how large the dark.

*

Whatever was struck in the storm burns
in the blind lull
left by a power failure. Dumb
when the telephone wires slack, we speak
somehow by their poles' slow smolder;
this is what our voices always wanted
to look like anyway.

*

A felled tree, wearing its latest ring,
points to me.
And so I marry disaster.

THE FIRST AMENDMENT TO THE CONSTITUTION OF THE UNITED STATES

The old Jew down the road near the grist-mill
died, call a *minyan*. Call ten men to howl
prayers into amber bottles, and with wood
mallets tap mourning-songs
from their transparent necks. And call the frogs;
the flies have been jewelling the wayside jackal
droppings, they glitter and make a sound of wire
plucked by the sun's touch; call blackwater frogs
and venus-flytraps carted over flagstone.
Also, call the caucus; and everyone playing faro
is welcome, even the croupier, tell her here
she could slither out of her glitter and run
on all fours with the rams and uproot cabbage.
Call the cows home. Call the reserves.
Dwarf-stars and snails are in alliance.
Tell the spelling-bee its napkins are folded
in hyacinth-shape on the plum-patterned plates.
Let them congregate; let them daisy-chain so dense
word travels from thighbone to thighbone
like code rapped through the length
of a blue metal bannister; let the space
between them be sweat; call the midgets;
ask the fife platoon; call the wranglers and glaziers;
if their brains are packed so flat together
one torched tongue arsons a flash-fire
under the scalp of the whole generation, yes,
though the word be "revolution," even if their souls'
metaphorical hands are twisting teeth from the gums
to hurl like stones through the corneal blind-spot:
call the cubs to the sows' teats, engrave what gulls

you may find along the abandoned pier
with my wedding invitation.
Let the sky go argyle with magpies.
Let the waters plump paisley with shrimp.
It begins.
Let the triplets be an ellipsis.

DEFEAT

1.
One day there's an object.
The next, you're under the object.

2.
That's not defeat. Defeat
is saying it, telling the mirror *I'm*
under the object. Perhaps there isn't anywhere
else to turn but to the razor,
like an ugly girl
it needs defeated men. That isn't kind,
I know, but the thought
puts back the *hone*
in *honest* we were frightened,
all these years, to pronounce.

3.
Well I don't know much about
thought. But the body
was made to want
to live. Just hold your breath till you die,
I'll say I told you so
at the eyelids' first faint prising.
Consciousness, little rabbi, marries
the lightless air in the skull
to a pekoe August sky. The honeymoon
sclera.

4.
I always thought defeat was a weight
on the back; but see now
it's a hole, an emptiness.

5.
In it goes the object,
a cornerstone; light, say,
in the pupil. And around it the iris and white
of new vision.

6.
Ugly girl,
I think I see your strategy,
loser, lover, wife.

PISCARY POEM

We fish,
for instance, for metaphors
as well as bluegills. Conceptual
and physical align, as if to say
the idea of piscine anatomy
and a flailing carp
fill the same clear space in lakewater.

I can see you, flesh pulled by the sun
out from your blouse-sleeves and rolled jeans-legs,
sprawl on the bank-edge, its trim, and troll
your pole-hand lazily back and forth;
the Western notion of female beauty lights
on your cheek like a sunrise; or it is
the sunrise. Is it real enough?

I invented it. You know we never fished
together, or ever even get much
out of the city limits: I fabricated the scene
to please you, and now can't get it out
of my head; and it fills my head
with a red light, a sunlight perfectly congruent
with my skull, as: who could say if it's blood

or love that really shapes the erection?
Both; and I bless them both for the license
they give me to sink in you, both ways
at once, like any solid noun
swimming up a simile, or a burning
proton of semen now synonymous with the dictionary
definition of intercourse, like this fish thriving

in fishing rights.

THE POEM THAT DOESN'T LOOK LIKE MUCH

for Sylvia

1.

You don't flaunt your diamonds,
not in Chicago. A leather loop
or string around the knuckle will do. And certain lovers
I know are accepting loss
as the least-ephemeral sign of their marriage:
a missing limb, a word repressed.
Another day in Chicago.

2.

Sure, sparrows survive. They're invisible. The ugly city
matches their dingy coats, when winter fades it a little
uglier—a sparrow's foreseen this, is chirping
unheard in an inner nook. And in the ugly city
Ring Man slips across a shadowed threshold, hangs
above the sleepers, twice
snips with his wire cutters and rides the rising scream
to safety with two new fingers
jiggling in his bag and two new bands for pawning.

3.

The Jewish groom
stamps, once, like that, on a glass
no larger than enough
to hold the first wet from both of them
on the honeymoon night. Once,
like that—she drinks,
he drinks, and when it's clear
it's cracked: its wine-color permanently
drawn into their flushing.

4.
And this is that poem. I know,
it doesn't look like much.

5.
But mutation's lasted in Quincy Forest Preserve
over generations, every year
the central meadow more drab. You go there
now, you find a ring of flowers
never to be vandalized: the ash-gray petals,
the total lack of perfume.

6.
The way, in these times, we have to blend
with the wall, some having adopted the habit
of wearing a necklace of edge-chipped bricks
or having a shattered back-window installed in their chests.
It isn't easy, but
we're safe. You look in such a window:
rows and rows
in the abandoned warehouse
where moths the color of iron ingots are draining
the last of their color
away. One flask of it goes
on the black market yearly.

7.
And this is the drop I've saved
for the toast
at our invisible wedding. This invisible flower
for my boutonniere—it cost
everything that bulges
my empty pockets. We're safe.

89

I love you. The blood and brown
in my eyes is being cried in a new direction,
drink it. I marry you. This shot-glass
—heavy, secretive, in the chest.

THE BITTERSWEET COMFORT OF MOTLEY DETAIL

In an open field, flat and clear for miles,
nothing is apparent. The sun's shine
is a matrix, steady, ubiquitous, some
insincere smile above a broad desk.
To wail into a sky with no borders
save those of the limits of vision
only extends the voice
into the province of blindness.
An honest sigh is delicate, skinned
like a little cloud, no bone, all juice;
and breathing it into that
landscape-without-detail is to lose it
with no chance for echo, reflection,
or cradling it to your breast.

the oil of fish; the oil of berries;
the thick lubrication of human grief;

In woods
the noon is still dim, and dense
enough for any scrape or overturning
to be revelation. The sun
between bunching bough-clusters shapes
its every unit like words of a secret.
This is it, written down.
This is what I learn today: one long light
armature in the world
around which the terrible Dark Machine
keeps turning, keeps fuelled, keeps up all night.

STRADDLING THE BANKS

The paper boats are the word: south.
Fish seem the shadows of birds.
The birds go: south.
The news is a day old and drying

out in the sun at some port a day away.
A child unfolds your craft,
the keel yesterday's war statistics, the sail
yesterday's beauty queen. The air says:

October, the world is moving
closer to the sun and growing colder.
The leaves in the current say: south.
Deer could bend to drink and give up

their lips to that wet pull.
The sun's too bright, it says look down
in water for what a mirror knows.
Your face is the one thing that falls to the stream

without loss.

SURVIVAL

This is the church of giraffes
dying on their knees, who cannot cry out
the length of their pain but must

topple silently, silently
as haunches unconnected to throats
attract carnivores, voiceless as offal.

This is the word they would say,
that rabbits begin with soft twitching
lips ceaselessly, but never finish

until their deaths; when the life
long stuttering of fragile and hesitant
f's: fulfills itself, once, unheard.

This is where we will marry, here
where the teat of the female buffalo hangs
its appendix weight; a hide-away

bed, safe in the walls, where I can love you
finally. Easily hovering overhead, cherubim
cannot appreciate the floorbound blessings

penguins offer: pumping, pumping vestigial
gestures for centuries, their strain inspires
one sublime squawk, long extinct from our language,

and keeps them warm till morning.

POEM TO COMFORT MY SISTER

1.
May wind
sets the edges of Chicago
fluttering, almost as if the city would lift
off the map and skitter
weightlessly, its zip codes tumbling
through metaphorical lottery drums.
May sun, May foam,
May high-tide lines
inched up the beach
in intersecting parabolas.
Gulls' beaks shear out
a perfect circle of air,
let it drop, stitch it back.
And I'm
eye-level with kiwis, feeling the world
smacked damp against my belly
catch the breeze
in a tremor that's what ruffling
is to a silk babushka.
This is the day
Chicago could snap its plumbing
and levitate,
tousled, transparent, if not for the hospitals,
*
funeral parlors, jailhouse backrooms
splattered with trachea-blood and spit,
marine recruiting centers, padlocked

orphanages with eyes inside window-glass
emblematic of burnt-out bulbs, insane
asylums, TB sanitariums shaking
a leaf in a cough, a tree of coughs, and every
darkened doorjamb waterlogged
with a wino's pea-colored phlegm
or hooker's nightly volume of ten-buck come
*

weighting down the city's corners.
Each rust-speck has its gravity.
And even then,
no babushka, a scrap of butcher-paper
perhaps, Chicago could shake itself
free for a moment and waft
up a manhole's steam
*

if I wasn't bent, pressed recklessly down
on all glass-lacerated fours,
the dirt beneath my fingernails
the heaviest thing in Illinois.

2.
This morning, a dream of our father
bloated, like pigskin, under the reaming-knife.
This evening, the trance, the stare-at-the-wall,
feeling each bit of dust
hit my shoulder, mote on mote
until it accretes
in its original shape as a bird
on a wire.
Every hour clicked off with the sound
of a respirator's surrender.
And

*
in the middle of today's whole fracas
I stopped at Juneway Beach to inhale
as much of the long wave-lapped horizon
as my chest could hold. I write this
to you knowing someday you'll ask me something
of getting through life, why it must be inch
by inch; and then I'll ask you to remember
this, how on an easier day, without a thought
of divorce court or caskets
clotting my mind, I kneeled in sand
as if to print a focal point
for the turning gulls; and, feeling the salt
brined up behind my eyes
in osmotic stability
with the salt air, I stared
down the undulating stretch of whatever
there is to breathe along the curve where water slaps sky,
and took my first
really cognizant lungfull,
and hoisted myself through this life
on a frayed rope of air,
a blue rope, unit by unit,
*
and each blue unit the length of my nostril,
and reeled the world's rim in.
This is the epoch of little miracles.
And if the traffic is punctuated with ambulances
and hearses splattering all day
like the death of a genus of insects
against our windshields, still
we musn't overlook to be wide-eyed and thankful
*
our retinas work at all.

97

3.
Ernest Vincent Wright lifts his pen
from the last wet word of the last strange page
of *Gadsby*, and sighs
through a smile. The word dries.
The year is 1939,
and he's just finished a novel
of over 50,000 words—not one
(and now the smile shapes
around the deep o's and a's
of a belly laugh) damn word containing
the letter e.

*

Now sound of bamboo on palm
poks through the forest. A Tasaday
swings his L-shaped bamboo mallet high
overhead, and poises
a glistening split-second
under the Philippines sun, then arcs
down hard, and smashes
the tasty *natok* starch from split palm.
Blows land daylong
less than a quarter-inch from his feet,
this being the way
his father taught him; that night
he squats in his cave niche,
removes the orchid-leaf loincloth
and gives his body over
to the wind's caress, his ten toes wiggling
a dance on their side
of the line between accuracy and crippling,
his tongue

revelling in a ball of cooked *natok,*
a small joy, a little precision.

*

And Brooks
drops asleep under sodium pentathol,
dreaming his guts
carved out, his rectum sewed
irreversibly shut, his body's stinks
collecting overnight from now on
in a plastic bag;
and wakes
colostomized in the bed
beside our father's,
to find himself again
not dead.

*

This is the epoch of little miracles,
Livia, take what you can get.
Gull, does your beak snip?
  —I surgery air.
Will it hurt?
  —The waves are anesthetists.
Sandpiper, sandpiper, drill me deep.
  —Fish-mouths are holes, but the lake goes on living.
Livia, don't be afraid.
Each time we feel the pain spade under our hackles,
something's working right.

4.
Listen:
Livia, don't be afraid.

One night, maybe, you'll wake to the cold
shoot of air across your shoulders
though the windows are locked. And then you mustn't
wring your sweat from the blanket-fringe
in fear, or think a touch like that anything
but my caress. It could be

*

one day you'll be walking the beach,
smiling, sneakered, hair amazed
in the wind, when you'll suddenly see yourself
against the blue
as if from a gull's perspective, and realize
how thin the cohesion
that keeps the atoms of your hand
from lifting into the air.
And you'll know lakewater
for what it is, a touch, maybe my touch
organized less tight;
you musn't tremble at this.
Or maybe
you'll thrust your arm in the air
and feel one atom
deep in your palm hum clearly
in affinity, and rise like carbonation
through your lifeline's crease, and free itself
into atmospherics;
and you'll walk on, aware, an isotope
of who you were
last minute. On a day like that
the edges of this smudgy city itself
could be so tenuous, lose themselves in brume,
metamorphose. Do you doubt
I'll be there to comfort you?

Listen:
even now the water's aerating
foam around sandpiper legs.
Slowly lift your fingers and scent
*
the gas you could be,
the light perfume.

FIELD

". . . there was always a spot which it was
forbidden to touch, or to walk upon. It was
dedicated to the gods—and especially evil
ones—in return for their implicit agreement
not to stray into provinces where they might
molest mankind. The same idea obtained
in parts of Scotland. Uncultivated pieces of
land were left fallow, and termed the 'guid
man's croft.'"

And this is that poem. Not much happens.
There are countless possibilities. I imbue
the poem with a solid man, and a hint
of woman (sometimes the reverse is true).
Not much happens. There are images,
small everyday ablutions, that are potential
strategies and symbols: he wanders
under moons and comets, his lungs full
with biological processes, fish, fruit,
or the probability of their disappearance,
the gesture of a pianist's wrist peaked
like a thoroughbred's foreleg, a dance
troupe in ritual circle (this is the female
entering the poem), the funeral, the children,
the mosque, the mask, the map, the home.
Not much happens. Anything can;
but this one I leave for tattered health,
mistallied votes, financial misfortune,

the ups and downs of sexual deprivation,
undernourishment, and overcaution:
unworked. Let this be my guid man's croft
that I will not finish or furnish or sign
with any name but my true name.
I leave it: propitiatory, begun, benign.